Stories of a Lost Sock

Zolton Kortvely
Illustrated by Jill Hummel

Stories of a Lost Sock

Published by Wheatmark®
610 East Delano Street, Suite 104
Tucson, Arizona 85705 U.S.A.
www.wheatmark.com

International Standard Book Number: 978-1-60494-059-6
Library of Congress Control Number: 2008921227

This book is dedicated to all the people who may
be in search of socks that have been separated
one way or another

and

to my family for all the support
that they have given me

4

I feel so sad and lonesome, because
I have to be alone.

My partner can't find me, because we were
separated during the washing and drying cycle!
The wash machine and dryer spin us so fast that
we get dizzy and lose our way.

Sometimes, we get mixed up with other clothes, and we are separated for many days. I wish we could always walk together with our friendly people!

We have quite a life keeping feet warm, but sometimes we don't smell so good, because our caretaker keeps using us for a long time.

Occasionally, we get paired up with a strange sock, and we are put in the dirty clothesbasket to await our fate!

Now the sad part of being a sock is when we suffer a hole in the toe and the owner puts us in the trash.

If you see a sock walking around by itself, feel sorry, because his partner is lost. If only I could make some noise so my partner could find me!

There are days that we are happy.
Especially when we get washed with nice soap
and warm water.

Then the real joy is when we get hung on the
wash line to dry in the warm sunshine and
gentle breeze. I wish they could make softer
clothespins, so they would not pinch!

One day while we were hung up to dry on the clothesline, a bird sat next to us and began pecking at us! I felt bad because I was in pain and part of me dropped to the ground. Nobody likes stringy socks!

Big fat feet are another problem, because people try to stretch and pull me on big feet. Nobody likes saggy socks!

There are times when I get shoved under the bed. I hate that because it's so dark and dusty and lonesome! I like to be with other socks, even without my partner.

I don't like sneakers because people use me as a sponge to soak up sweaty feet. The odor is simply terrible!

Why do I have so many problems?
All I want to do is fit snuggly and keep feet
warm and comfortable!

Why must I get lost?

Why must the birds pick on me?

Why must my caretaker wear me too long
and make me smell?

Why must I get holes because of sharp
toenails?

I guess I am just a lost and lonely sock...

But, at last! I find my partner and
we are a happy pair once again!

DATE DUE

Printed in the United States
117158LV00002B